T0368358

SHOCKWAVE

PETER R. SHAND

authorHOUSE

AuthorHouse™ UK
1663 Liberty Drive
Bloomington, IN 47403 USA
www.authorhouse.co.uk
Phone: UK TFN: 0800 0148641 (Toll Free inside the UK)
UK Local: (02) 0369 56322 (+44 20 3695 6322 from outside the UK)

Published by AuthorHouse 10/12/2023

ISBN: 979-8-8230-8231-0 (sc)
ISBN: 979-8-8230-8232-7 (e)

Library of Congress Control Number: 2023907295

Print information available on the last page.

Any people depicted in stock imagery provided by Getty Images are models, and such images are being used for illustrative purposes only. Certain stock imagery © Getty Images.

This book is printed on acid-free paper.

Because of the dynamic nature of the Internet, any web addresses or links contained in this book may have changed since publication and may no longer be valid. The views expressed in this work are solely those of the author and do not necessarily reflect the views of the publisher, and the publisher hereby disclaims any responsibility for them.

CHAPTER ONE

THE LAST MAN ON EARTH

Synopsis - A Comedy about a Scientist who's experiment creates a Shockwave that turns everyman on Earth into a Homosexual.

27 year old, Single, Lady, Tracy Styles moves into her brand new dream home. Tracy and her neighbour Sally don't get along from the start. A Month or so after moving in, During one hot Summer's Day, Tracy sees her neighbour Sally Hamilton kissing a Man. Tracy is putting out her washing. She is shocked because the Man Sally's is kissing isn't her Husband. Tracy tries to hide but it's too late. It's clear Sally knows she's been seen. That night Sally is forced to tell her Husband, Doctor Max Zero about the affair. She's leaving him for a Man called Ray Harms.

Max confines in his cleaner, Sharon Brookes. She's an actress and her first leading role is about a Woman in an physically, Mentally abusive relationship.

Sharon Brookes.

Max Zero's is his real name. He's a Genius. He's been recognise as such since he was a child. He's been on the Lowdown. He's excited because he's almost finished his new Project. It's called the Console.

The M1.

A Virus is a Sub microscopic infectious agent that multiply inside the living cells of an organism. Viruses infect all types of life forms, from Animals to Plants, All on a Microscopic level, The Console's aim is to kill certain Viruses such as the Ebola Virus. But there are other Viruses that grows within us.

1. Marburg virus.
2. Rabies.
3. HIV.
4. Smallpox.
5. Hantavirus.

Hormonal Changes, And Drug Use.

Women develop their breasts during puberty as estrogen increases. Pregnancy and milk production can also cause the breasts to enlarge due to hormonal changes. Certain drugs can lead to enlarged breast tissue in both Men and Women. Antidepressants known as selective serotonin reuptake inhibitors also enlarge breast tissue.

The Console.

This is a type of space invaders that Max has already completed. That's why Sally's bra has doubled in size. That's why she's taller than she was and why she never gets ill.

Hair Loss.

Level 27 is farming the Bacteria that controls hair growth. The aim is to prevent or encourage hair loss. Once gamers become accomplished they will be no need for shavers. If you become really good you will be able to make patterns in your hair, Simply from playing a computer game. One day this technology may even replace the need for a hair dressers.

The M1 - Space Invaders.

The Veins are the roads. Gamers drive in the Console aka the Body. The aim of level 11 is to protect White Bloods Cells. There are various Microscopic lifeforms that are helpful and dangerous. If mastered patients won't need Doctor's anymore.

Adults Only.

The Thalamus helps Translate information about touch, Movement, and any Sexual memories or fantasies. A Male or Female might be called upon to help them reach Orgasm. Meanwhile, The Hypothalamus is busy producing Oxytocin and may help co-ordinate arousal. Various levels offer a drug free, Natural mild stimulus that is harvested in the Console. Orgasms can only be achieved if an adult successfully completes the game.

Cancer.

Bacteria do not grow and multiply the same way as Animals or Humans. They take in nutrients and reproduce by dividing. This means one Bacteria splits and becomes two Bacteria, Two become four, Four become eight and so on. Doubling can occur quickly if the right conditions are met enough nutrients, Proper temperature and adequate moisture. The Bacteria multiply however the modern person can still clock the level.

Max Zero's younger Brother, Johnny visits to support him through the break up of his Marriage. Johnny instantly develops a crush on Max's new Neighbour, Tracy styles.

One evening Johnny Zero helps Sharon Brooke aka the cleaner to rehearse her lines. However Tracy thinks they're arguing in real life. The shocked Tracy listens to Johnny insult Sharon until she bursts into tears. That evening Johnny takes Max out to the local Pub.

Johnny drives home, Even though he is drunk. All goes well until he runs over Tracy's Dog and kills it. The poor Dog's name was Misty. He knocks her door and confesses to what he did and explained the situation. Then the drunk Astronaut Captain asks Tracy styles on a date. Not surprisingly Tracy makes it clear she wouldn't date Johnny if he was the last man on Earth.

Space Mission.

The rejection helps Johnny to decide to move out of his Brother's home but first he must go into space to fix a damaged Satellite.

Meanwhile.

Max Zero is not involved in the Space Mission. Not in person anyway. Johnny has a idea. He hacks into the Satellite Signal that the brother aim to fix. Max plans to adapt his new amazing game console software. He intends to use it to turn Trevor homosexual.

He types away on his computer and then presses execute. unfortunately for him he doesn't notice his cold fusion experiment has over heated. He was too preoccupied with his new twisted idea of revenge. It creates an massive explosion which kills him instantly.

Mission Controller Vince Calabri.

Johnny returns to Earth and as usual the gay mission controller flirts with him. It takes a while but he starts to realise every man has somehow been turned gay. He told the news about his Brother's a death. The heartbroken Johnny gains Max's house in the will. Obviously Sally is not too pleased that she didn't get the house. To make matters worse, Trevor leaves sally for another man.

Johnny continues to employ Sharon as his cleaner. He asks her to find out why Tracy hates him. Sharon says "You killed her Dog." Johnny says "She use to give me dirty looks before that." Sharon has a talk with Tracy. Tracy explains the argument she saw between her and Johnny. Sharon has to explain that Johnny was helping her with her lines. Tracy apologises to Johnny and she starts to help him through the death of his Big Brother.

It isn't long before romance is in the air. However lots of Women have started to hit on Johnny. Afterall he's the only straight Man alive. Tracy becomes jealous.

The Hat and Head Pub.

One evening Johnny takes Tracy to the local Pub. After a second glass of Wine Tracy confesses she once appeared on a talent show called Tune In. She is then encouraged to sing and she does. Hence forth Wednesday nights are Karaoke Nights.

Johnny agrees to help Tracy decorate but before he knows what's going on the Police raid Tracy's home. They arrest Johnny. Sally, Aka Max's ex Wife claims Johnny and Max are to blame for the reason why all the Men in the World have suddenly become Gay. She also insists they did it to ruin her new relationship with Ray Harms. She explains that she left Max for another Man. Fortunately there isn't enough evidence to keep Johnny in jail so the Police release him. But a few days later and the Government do confirm Max did cause the Homosexual crisis. Various countries decide to sanction English Products.

Johnny has brought a new Dog. He calls him Crisp. Owning a Dog encourages Johnny to flirt with Tracy. She's got a new Dog too. Her new Dog's called Sweetie. They walk their Dogs at the same time. Mornings, Noon and Night. Tracy tells Johnny he needs ten dates before they end up in bed for the first time. Their first real kiss happens in a Cinema during the Movie called A tearful kiss.

Synopsis - A Tearful Kiss.

The Story of a Woman who is granted the ability to turn her Husband into an an item of clothing.

The Next Day.

The American Government start to show subliminal messages during T.V advertisements. The Messages are sent as an attempt to cure Homosexuality.

The Politicians all over the World create a task force that they call the Alliance. They persuade the rest of the World to invade England within seven days unless they fix the crisis. They have evidence that they have seven more days before mankind is stuck this way forever. They have to fix it now or be stuck like this forever. Meanwhile Women of all shapes and sizes are offering to pay Johnny to be an escort.

New Mission.

Johnny has been told he must go into space to shutdown the corrupted Satellite. This may cause a reverse effect. This means everyone may go back to how they where before Max's Shockwave but Johnny might become Homosexual. Never the less captain Johnny Zero accepts the mission.

9th Date.

First they walk their Dog's then they go to an expensive Restaurant. They're next door neighbours. Should Tracy stop at Johnny's or should Johnny stay at Tracy?"

Paper, Scissors and stone - Johnny wins

He spends the night at Tracy's. She was making him wait before they took their relationship to the next stage. It's only been 5 dates, After all she may not get another chance with him.

The Next Day.

Johnny gets suited and booted. However the mission controller, Vince Calabri is planning to sabotage the mission. He is with Ray Harms Aka Sally's old Partner. He has put a banana in the tailpipe of the Space Shuttle. Fortunately he was caught on camera but they can't stop it now. They countdown from ten. 10.9.8.7.6 5.4.3.2.1 - Blast off.

Fortunately Johnny blasts into space and manages to shut down the signal of Max's satellite. Then as expected all the Men in the World who use to be Heterosexual turn back to being Heterosexual and all the Men who were already Homosexual simply carried on as normal.

But the question is has the self confessed ladies man, Captain Johnny Zero been turned gay? Tracy kisses him and asks him are you gay? He says "I don't know." He gets another kiss from Tracy, Johnny says "i'm still not sure, Give me one more kiss." She knows he isn't gay. They give each other a long kiss. The rest of the World call back their armies that had surrounded England. Finally Ray Harms gets back with Sally.

The End.

CHAPTER TWO

———•◆•———

DARKROOM

Clive Maxwell is a professional photographer. He occasionally gets to work with Glamour Models. Today is one of those days. His 11 o'clock booking arrives. Her name is Easter Anderson. Clive struggles to move his large, Brand new, Top of the range lighting equipment. It was delivered that weekend. The shoot finishes at 1 pm. Instead of going home, Clive goes straight to his Darkroom.

The Shockwave.

Clive is a freelance Photographer. He's offered a new job. He'll be taking photographs of Male and Female Models. The Photoshoot will be on Tally's Golf course at 10 pm. Clive excepts once he finds out it's for one of the top Magazines. The Shockwave hits as if it's a storm but Clive continues the shoot. However. From nowhere he's struck by lighting several times.

Stella Peterson.

Clive wakes up refreshed, Bright and early the next Morning. Instead of home, He goes straight to his Studio. His new client arrives at 9 am. He moves the lights to a new part of his office. The client says "You should get a trolley or something to make moving that easier. It can't be good for your back." Clive says "it's not heavy." He lifts it up with one hand.

The Model says "Wow it looks heavy." She walks over and tries to lift it but she cant. She can barely move it at all. She says "i'm only a Girl." She raises her eyebrows as if she's impressed. She flirts with Clive throughout the shoot.

At the end of the Session he walks Stella to the exit. It's obvious she wants him to make move. He asks her if she wants to do something. A restaurant or a Movie? She says "Yeah. You've got my number, Call me." She stays stood as if she wants him to make a move. His eyes widen when he cottons on. They kiss for a short while, Clive has a session with a Model called Easter Turner at 11 pm. So they can't go any further.

The Next Day.

Clive has a photo shoot with Stella Peterson. She doesn't turn up, She also doesn't answer his phone calls. Clive goes to Mark Hamlet's House. They've been best friends since Junior School. Clive tells Mark about the Model called Stella. He simply assumes she got cold feet. Stella's agent paid up front for the Photoshoot so he's got the Morning free. Mark's sister Rukia over hears them talking. She reminds Clive that he offered her a free Photoshoot. Does it still stand? Clive has a big time crush on Mark's younger sister. He says "yes."

Rukia makes Mark take a photo of her new pet hamster, Spot. Unfortunately she gets a phone call from her Boss. Rukia's a Nurse so she needs to work at short notice. It's 5 pm, Clive's new client is due soon. Her names Karen Humphrey. Clive moves the lights again. This time with no strain at all. He knows something strange is happening.

Test After Test.

He's forced to admitt to himself, He has developed super strength. It's 6:30 pm, The Police raid Clive's Studio. P.C Ralph Gadge informs Clive that Stella Peterson has been reported Missing. She missed her Mother's Birthday Party. Stella organised it. She also missed an important meeting with her agent. Clive says "She missed a meeting with me too." Clive shows PC Ralph Gadge his appointment book. "We were going to do a shoot at the Central Gardens." Clive says "When you see her tell her I don't give refunds."

Super Hero.

Clive wants to be a Super Hero. He buys a pair of tights but decides to wear jeans, Once he sees how silly he looks in tights. He rushes out and buys the coolest gothic clothes he can find. Once home he tries on his full outfit. The doorbell rings. It's P.C Ralph Gadge again. Clive takes off the hoody. He's still dressed as a super hero. Easter Turner has also Gone missing. Ralph wants to arrest Clive but he has evidence.

That Night.

Clive rushes to Mark's House. He tells him the full story. He even lifts Mark's Dads car up off the ground. Mark has a theory. "Maybe you was effected by the lighting strikes. Maybe it was the camera. Some Third World Cults believe cameras steel a person's soul." He remembers Clive took a Photograph of Spot. They brake into Rukia's Bedroom. Spot still is his cage.

Rukia catches them in her room. They've forced to tell her the whole story. Clive proves he has super strength by lifting all of Marks weights. He tells them he's not going to do anymore Photoshoots until he sure his camera isn't killing anyone. If it's me spot will disappear too. We'll give it a week or so.

That night Clive fantasises about Rukia but every so often a different Model pops into his mind. Clive calls Mark first thing the next Morning. Spots fine. Clive gets a visit from P.C Gadge. A Man has confessed to killing the Models. His names is Adam Jones. P.C Gadge asks "Do you know him?" Clive says "No.

Clive has been cancelling all his appointments. He calls several Models, Male and Female. He also contacts a family who were set for a Family Portrait. That Morning P.C Gadge got a Message. Adam Jones aka the Man who confessed to killing the Models, He's been killing female dogs. That's why he's been calling them Bitches. It's a Saturday, Clive gets back to work. He reschedules the Family portrait for 5 pm.

Short Notice.

First, Clive has a photoshoot with Beth Stapleton. Everything goes smoothly. She asks if he's O.K doing Sexy lingerie? He says "Yes." Beth Stapleton is a friend of Stella Peterson. She's a Model too. Clive needs his lights. He uses the trolley. Beth asks "Are those lights heavy?" Clive says "Yes. That's why I use this trolley. It has a brake on it. I look like I can move it with my bear hands. This is a trick to impress Women." He tells Beth to try to move the lights. She does.....easily. She asks "Why are you telling me?" Clive tells her about Stella and his other Models.

That Night he planned on restarting his second job as a Super Hero. But he gets some bad news. Spot the Hamster has disappeared. He rushes to Mark's House. Mark had put a camera in Spot's cage. The Hamster slowly disappears over a few minutes. It happens once Spot goes to sleep. Tracy smashes Clives Camera.

Mark explains his theory. If you continue making photocopies of old photocopies eventually you'll be left with plain paper. Only the original won't fade. The concept that taking a photo of someone could fade them isn't realistic. "I wouldn't believe it if hadn't seen it with my own two eyes." No one else will either. And you've broke my camera. Clive says what if i'm the cause?

Mark says "Maybe your body has become a darkroom. It happens once you close your eyes at night. You start to develop other peoples life's into your system. That's why your getting stronger." Clive says "I think I'm going to be sick." Mark asks "What do you think about at night?" Rukia punches him on the arm. She asks Mark "What do you think about at night?" Mark nods to himself. He says sexual arousal isn't a factor hear.

Clive asks again "What if I'm the cause?" Rukia Carmly says "Well find a way to stop you from being able to hurt anybody. Don't worry no one is going to hurt you if I can help it." Clive cancels all his appointments by text. He points out that a few of his clients have gone missing. A serial killer maybe targeting him. So it's best to be on the safe side.

Cold turkey.

Clive goes to sleep early that night. It's 1 pm. He's had another nightmare. He's hungry but he can't digest normal food. It makes him sick. He's become addicted to what ever he gets from taking photographs. He tries to fight it but it's stronger than he is. He heads out and starts taking photographs of random people. They vanish straight away A Body Builder isn't too please when Clive takes a photograph of his Girlfriend. He tells Clive to delete the photograph. Clive says "No," He simply laughs and walks away.

The Body Builder calls the Police. He takes off his coat and chases after Clive. He pushes him as if he's wants to start a fist fight. Clive lifts him up with one hand and says "You'll loose." He puts the Bobby Builder down. Clive takes a photograph of him.

Clive sees a pretty young Woman. Unfortunately she's with someone too. Clive tries to claim the attractive Woman as if he has Alpha Male rights. She says "No". Clive sucks his teeth at her and heads back into the Town.

It's Friday Night.

Rukia has just finished her latest shift at the Hospital. She see's Clive taking photos. He's got a masked on but she recognises him. Clive only taking photo's of Men with Muscles and the prettiest Girls. She doesn't hesitate in calling the Police. No one paid any attention to the Boddy Builder, Not even the Police. But they listen to Rukia.

Come Quietly.

The Police find Clive, However he refuses to be apprehended. Ten Police officers try but they can't hold him down, Not even when they tackle him all at the same time. Clive sends them flying, left to right. P.C Gadge Refuses to use Lethal force. He urges everyone to keep their guns in there holsters. Rukia tries to calm Clive down. It doesn't work. She phones Mark. She tells him that "Clive has lost controll of his mind." Mark has an idea of how to stop him.

Clive steals a car. He drives away. Mark knows where he's going. Mark tells Rukia, Clive's heading for the Impact Telescope. The Army are waiting. They beat Clive there by using a Helicopters and Motorbikes.

The Impact Telescope Laboratory.

Rukia asks Clive to "Stop." He says "I can't she asks "What are you going to do? He says "I'm so hungry. I need to take a Photograph of a larger area. If that don't work i'll take a photograph of the far side of the Earth, If that don't work ill take a Photograph of the Sun. Don't worry i'll make sure your O.K." Mark phones his Sister, He asks "Is it working?" She says "Yes." Mark has burnt all of Clive's recent Photographs. Clive start to feel weak. Clive takes Photographs of all the Police. He even takes a Photograph of the helicopter. The Pilot Vanishes, The Helicopter crashes to the ground. Clive brakes into the Impact Telescope Laboratory. Rukia changes her mind. She tells Mark It isn't working. It's simply making him want more.

Clive pauses, He isn't going to take a Photograph of the other side of the Earth. The Impact Telescope doesn't work. It has a label on it. It says "Repairs will start next Monday." Clive fixes it. He takes a photograph of a star. It disappears. The whole Orion constellation vanishes. The Police arrive. This time they're willing to shoot to kill. Clive surrenders. He asks what have I done? He takes a photograph of himself. He simply disappears. The Police release Clive's victims and Orion belt. He eats food by taking Photographs eg chicken, Fish not People.

A Week Later.

The Phenomenon is blamed on the strike of lighting. However there's an underground section of the Goverment who know there's more to this story. This was connected to the Shockwave that turned everyman in the World into Homosexuals. This was an aftershock. experts confirm their will be other strange incidents like this.

The End.

CHAPTER THREE

News.

The Shockwave struck last night. Children and adults all over the country try to see if they have gained super natural powers. At this point their hasn't been any reports of unusual events even after last nights Shockwave.

Other News.

A Woman's body was found in Hipton Woods, Birmingham this Morning. She has been identified as 29 year old Amber Dean. She was well known by Police who had arrested her several times for Prostitution. The Murderer is still at large.

The News.

Last night a Goverment research laboratory was all but destroyed by Arsonists. The Birmingham Police believe the culprits are a suspected animal right group known as Fetch. They have yet to claim responsibility for the attack that cost three lives.

Why Do Terrorists Become Terrorists?

Those who engage in terrorism may do so for purely personal reasons, based on their own psychological state of mind. Their motivation may be nothing more than hate or the desire for power.

Fetch.

Jamie says "We need to choose a new target.

Top ten Places most at risk to terrorist attack.

1. Zhangye Danxia Geopark, China.
2. Venice, Italy.
3. Banff National Park, Canada.
4. Great Ocean Road, Australia.
5. Machu Picchu.

Jamie watches a program. It's about Billionaire Jordan Fortune. He's sells Guns to Third World countries. He's our new target. Amy reminds everyone that no one should get hurt. We give the Police a one hour warning. We only work at night so the building should be empty.

Work.

Stanley Francis visits his option aka Doctor Chris Winkler. Stan aka is told he needs glasses however he decides on contacts. A new retina scanner has been installed at the Skypool research laboratory. Unfortunately it keeps malfunctioning. A Scientist called Tom Joiner uses it b4 Stan. The retina scanner stalls before it recognises him. Stan registers straight away. He walks in 1 direction Tom walks in another. The lift sends Stan to the wrong floor. He's sure he presses floor 5. He's told the malfunction is due to a system crash. It's effected more than the retina scanner. It's effected all the other electrical systems in the research lab.

Night shift.

Stan studies a broken surveillance monitor. M4 keeps switches on and off. He makes a note of it. Amazingly it starts to show footage of a couple making love. Stan recognises the woman on the M4 monitor. It' Melissa Joiner aka Toms wife. Sure enough when the love making is complete Stan sees Tom looking at himself in a mirror. Stan cant believe his eye's Somehow he can see through the eyes of Tom. How is this possible.

That Morning, Volumtrous, Receptionist called Tabitha Racley wakes only to find her bra size has grown over night. From a 36D to a 36DD. Tabitha's boobs are so enormous she almost can't drive her car. She makes an appointment to see Doctor Duncan, Her G.P. Afterward she goes to work. Today is the day of the big presentation.

Amy Hicks

Tabitha cries on Amy shoulder. Amy asks if she can get time off work? Her line Manager aka Amy Hicks says "Your circumstances are extreme enough for you to be allowed sick leave. You've obviously been effected by the Shockwave.

Frank Case is the Day time Security Guard. He's watching the surveillance monitors. When Receptionist Tabitha enters the Office the 4th monitor switches on. It's clearly allowing Frank to see through the eyes of another person. That man is billionaire Jordan Fortune.

Jordan Fortune's company is promoting a safe sex campaign. He suggested they use Astronaut Captain Johnny Zero as the face of the project. But a Woman would also be useful. Even though he doesn't have any specific Woman in mind. Not until Tabitha enters the presentation room. He already believes in fate. He insist Tabitha's work on the project should be as a Model instead as a Administrator.

Game - Captain Johnny Zero and The S.T.D's

A malfunction increases the size of S.T.D's. to the size of an average Man. The S.T.D's leader, Bear Back's aim is to stop Men and Women from enjoying a healthy Sex life. Captain Johnny tries to stop the sexually transmitted disease aka Steedies.

3 Day's Later.

Stan Rowling is a voyeur. He's no longer doing his job properly. Meanwhile Frank aka the day time security guard has applied for a transfer to the nightshift. The Boss offers Stan the transfer. Stan point blank refuses it. He knows exactly why Frank want's to switch shifts.

That night Frank goes to work. He asks Stan "Why don't you want to transfer?" In a threatening manner. Stan says "The night shift is more money. Frank seems angry and frustrated. He asks again. "You do the day shift and i'll do the night shift?" Stan says "No thanks." Frank says "How much? I'll give you the extra money. Stan says no means no. Suddenly monitor 4 switches on. It isn't long before the bedroom fire works start.

Donna Fox - The Dinner Lady.

Frank Prayor already knew sexural arousal triggers the monitor. Stan's figured it out too. Monitor 4 switches on. They're able to recognise the Dinner Lady's Husband and their living room. Frank has his DVD Recorder. Stan says "Don't do that, It's bad enough were watching them but recording them is even worse." Frank pays no attention to Stan. The larger Man presses record. After Donna's night of passion is over, Frank checks his DVD Player. It's managed to record the footage. Suddenly the monitor switches off. They steer at it waiting to see if something happens. It switches back on again. A Woman is cuffed to a headboard. Then she is stabbed to death

They couldn't see who committed the Murder. But it was probably someone to do with the Captain Johnny Zero Project. Stan says "We all know each other, We have done for year's. There Strangers and all of a sudden there's a Serial Killer." Frank beggs Stan not to go to the Police. Stan asks "What kind of Security Guard are you?" "It's ours" says Frank. "Lets at least watch it until we've seen Tabitha. Stan says "No i'm phoning the Police." Frank threatens Stan. He throws Stan against the wall and says "it's ours. It's the Police's job to catch the killer not ours."

Karla Grants - Accountant.

She pull's a random Man at Club Fire in Broad Street, Birmingham. Frank says "Seeing it from her perspective isn't as good. He stops eating his popcorn.

Upgrade.

Retina system is having a World Wide Database upgrade. Everyone in the World will be registered. All visitors will be identifiable. It will improve all avenues of practice. The Government wants a copy of every citizens Retina scan. At the moment they only have 80%

Morning.

Frank asks Stan to record Monitor 4's events but he refuses. This means Franks forced to work all day, Watch the events of Monitor 4, Then sleep a few hours until he goes back to work.

Friday Night.

Franks drinking a beer even thought it's against the rules. It's 11.32 pm when Monitor 4 switches on. A couple are kissing in the woods. Suddenly the Women is punched to the ground and then she's strangled to death. Stan can tell it happened in the woods near the research Laboratory. He runs to the woods in the hope of stopping the Murder but it's too late.

Morning News.

The last Murder victim was a prostitute called Penny Montrose. She was only 19 years old. Frank starts to interrogate the members of staff he works with. Stan wonders, Could the Serial Killer be a Woman? What about his ex girl friend aka Theresa Woods.

Theresa Woods.

Stan hasn't noticed that she still has feelings for him. He asks her out on a date. He doesn't beat around the bush. He asks question after question. Are you single for example? She says "No i'm not single." Her Boyfriend's a white Man, He's 30 years old, He's always abroad on business trips and He lives in Birmingham, Jewellery Quarter. Stan doesn't think she's guilty but her Boyfriend might be. During the main course he asks "If I was a Murderer would you hand me in to the Police? Theresa says "Yes."

She asks "Are you telling me your the Serial Killer who Murdered those Prostitutes?" Stan says "No." Theresa asks do you think my Boyfriend is the Serial Killer? Stan says "Maybe."

7:00 pm.

After dinner she invites him into her home for coffee. He asks coffee, Is that all? They dated for two years before she ended it. Mainly because she got cold feet. She's still comfortable around him. She tells him "You can stay the night if you want." He says "No" because he's got to go to work. Plus another Security Guard would watch them.

The Next Day - Michael Austin. Cleaner.

This is who Stan suspects. The main suspect would of been Frank but it can't be him. Michael is always saying he hates Women. Last week in the dinner canteen he said "Just take a look at that Tabitha Racley's. She's all wrong. What are us Men suppose to do. Were full blooded Men. Being single isn't right, It's cruel."

Scott Naylor.

Frank thinks Scott Naylor is the Serial Killer. Stan thinks Scott's a player not killer. It's 2:00 pm, Frank says he's just been talking to Scott. Frank's sure Scott is the Serial Killer. Without warning Frank says "I'm not doing this anymore. I'm married. What if monitor 4 stops working. We'll end up in a Mad house. It's all yours."

Stan isn't sure what to do. The first victim was Scottish. The second victim was Scottish too. Stan talks to himself. He says "Just because his names Scott don't mean he goes around killing Scottish Women. Last night Frank accepted what Stan said but he still insists the killer is Michael.

It's 6 o'clock. Stan goes to Scott's house. Before he knocks the door he phones Frank. Scott's bigger than Stan. Scott answers the door. He offers to make Stan a cup of tea. Stan has a gun. Scott confesses to the Murders.

Stan phones Frank again. He gets no answer so he phones the Police. Scott Naylor is arrested. Stan phones frank but again he get's no answer.

7:00 am.

Stan is at work. He gets a phone call from the Police. Frank has been Murdered. Stan "Asks was it Scott?" The Policeman says "We don't know." The Murderer took both of his eye balls. The Policeman asks "Do you know why Scott would do that?" Stan says "I think he knew we were onto to him."

1:00 pm.

They empty Frank's locker. Stan's relaxed because Frank had deleted all his tapes. Stan tells Theresa he knew Scott was the Murderer. He used his magic Monitor. He invites her to his office.

It's 8 o'clock, The buildings is empty. Stan is telling Theresa how he caught Scott. Apparently Scott had killed 11 Women, All Scottish. He tries to prove his story is true by kissing her passionately. She lets him kiss her and more. Monitor 4 switches on.

9:00 pm, Stan receives another phone call from the Police. The Policeman asks him if he knows why Scott would take out Frank's eyes? Stan says "Scott knew we were onto him." It was a message......What you looking at?"

There's A Power Cut.

It's the Animal rights group, Fetch. They are the Terrorists who Murdered Frank. The Boss is called Jamie Carlson. He doesn't want to give warnings. His Girlfriend sees Frank's eyes. She argues but Jamie is in charge. Frank's eyes gets them pass the Retina Scanner. The upgrade still isn't finished.

Stan patrol's the Laboratory and notices the Terrorist are setting up a bomb. Stan phones the Police. He rushes into the Laboratory saying freeze. The Terrorist don't have guns. They stop and they tell Stan "We have four bombs. You should leave while you can. Stan makes sure the building is empty. He sets off the fire alarm. Stan points his gun at the five unarmed Terrorist. Stan calls the Police again. He's been spotted by Jamie. He does have a Gun.

Jamie enters the Laboratory. He says "Another bomb will go off in five minutes. Theresa creeps up behind Jamie. She pretends to have a gun. She pushes it into his back. She tells Jamie to throws his Gun to Stan. Jamie says "There are two minutes until the next bomb detonates." Stan, Theresa and the Terrorist run out of the building. Jamie simply stands there.

The Policemen and Firemen enter the burning Building. Jamie runs away but he's caught by his Girlfriend. She says "No one dies, That's the rule." She hands him to the Police. They arrest Jamie. It takes an hour before the power is switched back on.

The Next Day.

Jordan gives Stan permission to throw Monitor 4 away. The new Monitor 4 works normally. Stan watches all night for a week. The old Monitor 4 is thrown in the tip, However Stan brings it home, At 11:00 pm Monitor 4 switches on. It's Tabitha with Billionaire, Jordan Fortune.

The End.

CHAPTER FOUR

BRINK

Synopsis

Raylene Kaur is effected by the shockwave that hit's London City. If she see's a person in black and white it means they have less than an hour to live.

The news warns people not to look directly at the Sun during today's Solar Eclipse. If you do want to view it wear protective special glasses. Ash Peters is well known for throwing parties for almost any occasion. So it was obvious she was going to throw a Shockwave/Solar Eclipse Party. Ash is visited by the Neighbour's Cat, Monty. He knows how to ring the bell. Ash gives him a cuddle and a treat. Raylene Kaur asks if she can watch Ash's pirate copy of The Nymph Forrest.

The Nymph Forrest - Synopsis.

Hayle the Nymph has lost the ability to turn into a Christmas Tree. She knows the longer she spends as a Human the harder it will be to turn into a Tree.

Ash tells everyone the Solar Eclipse has started. They all rush outside. Raylene was about to watch the Movie. She grabs her glasses and rushes outside. Unfortunately she picked up the 3d glasses by mistake. The

Shockwave produces several solar flares. Everyone's eyes were hurt however Raylene was affected the worse. She instantly went blind.

Hospital.

Raylene says she can see strange glowing lights. Almost like it's the Aurora. Ash says "Sightings of the Aurora are common now. In any country and any major City.

The Doctor says "The rods in your eyes are damaged. However the cause is acute angle-closure glaucoma. You will be OK in a Month." Her temporary blindness explains why she started to suffer with Migraines.

Self Defence?

Ash feels guilty so she Volunteers to look after Raylene. She reads her a letter from her Boyfriend, Daniel Tralles. He's got sent to prison for 5 years. Raylene was getting stalked by her ex, Barry. Her current Boyfriend, Daniel confronted him and it turned into a fight. Barry claimed he carried a knife for protection. "If I had a Gun, I could use it for protection........if I lived in America." He excused Daniel of stealing his Girl. Daniel has a reputation. He got hold of the Knife. He was forced to use it once Barry started getting the upper hand. Daniel has severed five years of his ten year sentence.

Two Month Later.

Raylene can see again. She starts flirting with Doctor Patrick. She also tells Ash off for not telling her that Doctor Patrick was good looking. Ash says I shouldn't need to....his a Doctor. All Doctors are hot."

Back Home.

At first it feels like a strangers house but it isn't long before she settles back in at home. Ash offers to take care of her because she still suffers with Migraine but Raylene insists she's fine.

Shopping.

She amazed to see a Man appear in black and white. He's appearance seems to aggravate her Migraine. The stranger is greeted with a kiss by a Woman. She's like everybody else. She's in full colour. The couple go into a posh underwear shop. Raylene follows them. Why is he in black and white? The Woman is trying on some expensive lingerie. She calls her Boyfriend to check her out.

Raylene even browses at a few outfits herself. From nowhere she hears four gunshots. The Man in black and white is on the ground. He's been shot four more times. The shooter asks "Was that the Man you left me for?" The semi naked, Crying Woman yells "Yes." He threatens to shoot her too. He points the Gun at her head. The moment lasted at least a Minute. Then he simply runs away.

Raylene doesn't tell the Police. They would lock her up in a Mad House, For sure. Regardless of the recent Shockwave incidents. Raylene goes home still in shock. She can't believe a Man would kill over Woman.

Football - A Week Later.

Raylene goes to a football match with Ash and Ash's Boyfriend, Micheal. It's England vs Wales. Everything is going well. Raylene Volunteers to get the food and drinks. Her, Ash and Michael were talking about Love. Ash says "Relationships mainly work when a Man is too good for his Girlfriend." Michael agrees."

All of a sudden Raylene sees 1 person in black and white then 2 then 5 then 10 then more than meets the eye. She doesn't want to sound like a Mad Women but she tries to tell everybody that there's going to be an accident. She phones the Fire Brigade. She drags Ash and her Boyfriend Michael out of Wembley Stadium. Not long after a bomb detonates in the Visitors area. Thousands die.

The Next Morning.

Raylene see's the Neighbour's Cat. It's in black and white too. She looks at herself in a mirror.....She's in colour. She phones Ash and tells her, Monty the Cat is in black and white. Raylene looks outside as the Cat crosses the road. She hears the Cat scream as if it's hit by a Car. She rushes outside and see's the black and white Cat, Dead. She tells her Neighbour the bad news. For the rest of that day Raylene searches the net for unexplained phenomenon related to the Sun. Northing helps.

Visiting Day - Prison.

Raylene waits in the reception area. She actually knows 2 or 3 of the other visitors. She doesn't hesitate to tell Daniel the strange things that have happened to her. He seems preoccupied.

She says "I think I can see when someone is about to die." Daniel interrupts. He tells Raylene to leave because some of the prisoners have planned to riot. She is persistent Avisitor screams. She saw a spider. Raylene points at the spider. She says "It's in black and white. From nowhere a prison Officer called Kieran steps on it. He sits back down. Daniel is surprised. He says we'll have to talk about it another time. It's not safe. But it's too late.

The top dog of the Prison, Dennis Durie leads the Prison Riot before anyone has a chance to leave. They tried to tell their Girlfriends about the Riot but Women paid no attention.

Fred is 40 years old. He killed his own Dad over his inheritance/will. He's a hard knock. In fact he's second in line. He takes the Women into the reception area. Jessica Matton is visiting her Bank robbing Brother. She over heard Raylene talk about her ability to see if something is about to die. She asks Raylene "How did you gain the ability?" Raylene says "Probably the Shockwave but it could be from the solar eclipe." Jess asks Fred if she can have a word with the Boss aka the Shark.

Jess is taken to the Warden's Office. Before she tells him anything she makes him promise to look after her little brother, Wayne. The Shark agrees so Jess tells him about Raylene's ability. Obviously he doesn't believe a word of it however he's not about to pass up a trump card or a good hand. he tells her "I'll soon know if it's true or not." Jess asks "How are going to test her?" The Shark says Russian roulette.

He gathers a load of syringes. He also steels a box of tekosen and Hinerox. These medicines are used to put violent inmates to sleep. A small amount is enough to do the job however the Shark fills 10 syringes of tekosen and Hinerox. This mixture will definately kill. He also fills 10 syringes with upgraded methodone. He tells four prisoners to get Raylene. The Shark does his thing. He hardly ever looses.

He mixs 100 syringes and tells Raylene to point at the one with Methodone. She looks at her hand as she touches the syringes. She's turned into black and white. She looks at each syringe. She stops once her hand turns back into colour. She points at the syringe. The Shark injects her and waits. Raylene starts to feel the Methodone take effect. The Shark's left hand man aka Bruce Berry laughs at him and clap for Raylene.

The Shark gets another syringe with Methodone in it. Raylene points at syringe after syringe. She says "Who wants to Party?" She starts to dance. She can just about stand up. The Shark throws a whole box full of syringe on the table. There must be 99 syringe full of poison only 1 holds Methodone. Raylene points at one syringe. The Shark laughs as Raylene passes out. He lets her sleep it off.

5:00 pm.

Raylene is sent back to the Reception area, As soon as she wakes up. The first thing she does is punch Jess. It's obvious, She told the Shark about her Powers. Jess appologises and says "I did it for my little Brother. He's weak even I can beat still him up." Raylene laughs until the Shark's right hand Man aka Fred Barnes enters the Reception area. He drags another Woman out. Jess says "If Wayne is involved i'm finished with him for good."

The Raid.

The Police raid is postponed. The Shark calls for Raylene. She tells him he's is in black and white. He tells her "The Police will never take me alive."

Meanwhile - Hide and Seek.

Wanye tells Daniel the Shark has Raylene as a hostage. Daniel beats up any of the Shark's Men who try to stand in his way. They're preparing to fight in the Police raid. They have hostages, visitors and staff. The Police must back down. Daniel heads for the Warden's room but stops when he hears a Woman crying. Daniel enters meeting room 5. The Sharks number three is trying to rape a Woman, Staff not Visitor. Daniel knocks him out. Lots of Women see Daniel. He's holding hands with a Woman. Soon there are other Women following him. They're are another 10 Women hiding as if the Prison is a maze. That's why Fred is releasing the Women. Wayne follows Daniel too.

Daniel Vs The Shark.

Daniel makes it to the Warden's Office. It's locked until he kicks it open. Fred sees Daniel with the Women, He hides. Meanwhile there's a stand off in the Wardens office. Daniel and the Shark have respect for one another. Daniel calls the Shark, Adam. Daniel says "We've been best friends since they were children." They stand face to face like boxers. The Shark says "We waited long enough, To see who's number one." But Daniel steps aside so the Women can beat the living daylights of him. When the Women are finished. He asks "Don't let them take me alive"

The Shark puts the syringe to his arm and injects himself. He falls to the ground, Dead. They wait in the Wardens Office while the riots peters out. Raylene says "We're in colour. We're as safe as Houses." We're OK for another hour. "Is that how long it lasts asks Daniel?" Raylene's "Yes." The Police enter the Warden office. Daniel is arrested, A week later

He's released. The Women Daniel saved put a good word in for him and so did the Warden. He had been handcuffed to a radiator in the main hall.

6 Weeks Later.

It's late, Daniel and Raylene drive around the City. She see's a man standing on a bridge. He's in black and white. Raylene sits on the bridge next to him. They start to talk to each other until he turns into colour. again.

The End.

CHAPTER FIVE

————◆◇◆————

ESCAPE FROM NEW YORK

20 years ago Europe invaded the U.S.A. The Wall that separated them from Mexico only made them more isolated. Some English speaking Countries have had enough of learning English. Their ethos was, If we learn your language you can learn ours. All the other influential countries of the World had decided to band the English language. England had no option but to join U.S.A. Their reluctance to join with Europe led to a separation, And Economic Depression.

The Forth Of July.

At first Mexico supported the War against English language. But after years of separation, They joined with the English speaking nations of the World. Especially U.S.A. 30% of Mexicans are against the English language.

Vietnam Invades U.S.A.

They're supported by Europe and various other Countries. Including various Commonwealth countries.

- Greenland.
- Nicaragua.
- Honduras.
- Cuba.

All for the English Language. The World's only super power isn't a Country. It's not even a continent. It's a Language Barrier. None English speaking countries practically declare War on England and the other Counties that speak English.

Tech - A Teleporter.

A Welsh Scientist invented teleportation 15 years ago. But his laboratory was raided. His invention was stolen by a Non English speaking Nations. The French King summons the English Queen to the Palace of Versailles. The French King aka Gabriel de France Says "I heard the host of a quiz show called "Pocket Full" "He blatantly spoke English." He's been arrested."

Time Travel.

The English Queen can speaks French. She asks "Why are you talking in English? She says "Nous nous rendons" aka "We surrender" Time Travel was invented 10 years ago by a U.S scientist. The English aren't allowed to use it. Death is no longer salvation to English Language countries." The 21 year old Queen would rather be dead than be with 40 year old French King.

- China,
- The Gambia, Malawi,
- Colombia,
- Swaziland,
- Brazil,
- Russia,
- Argentina,
- Algeria,
- Uganda,
- Yemen,
- Chile
- Tanzania.

The Forth Reich.

These countries have decided to join forces with Germany's forth Reich. Aggression is triggered to any person who speaks English.

Obviously there are various Countries that Would joined the attack on the English language but still shun Germany.

Buckingham Palace.

English people aren't free. They can't speak the English language in public. They're treated like Black citizens in South Africa, During the apartheid culture or Jews in Nazi Germany.

The France King asks what does this mean in English "tu deviendras un esclave insensé or vous deviendrez esclave conscient. Cest ton choix. The Queen translates it. "The French King says come here...my Wife to be. The English Queen says "I'm not your wife in French "Je ne suis pas ta femme."

The Grapevine - News Paper.

Jamaica join forces with Briton. Spain say Jamaica are biting the hand that feeds them. Back page. Liverpool F.C win the Champions League again.

The Freedom Community.

Our community members mirror the ethos of great revolutionaries past and present. We only welcome those who uphold the teaching of great Men and Women such as Martin Luther King, Mother Theresa, Ghandi or Nelson Mandela. We will only use the most eco friendly of modern devices. We aim to be one of the most technological communities in the World. We aim to encourage our community members to create less dependency to cultures with separate values than ours. We do have church's and other Religious buildings. However we all prey to God.

The Million Man March - The Freedom Community.

It's to be held in London. Some shops have to close, Because they lost their staff. It's for English Language speakers. They're 100 Police making sure the march doesn't turn into a riot

Monday Night - The Meek Foster School. Dwayne is top of the Class. He's top of all his classes.

Shockwave.

The Parents who live in the Freedom Community send their children to these types of Foster Homes. Dwayne is watching T.V. when the Shockwave strikes. He knows instantly. He has gain super intelligence. The Host of the game show asks name top ten tech that has never been invented in real life

Top ten best inventions.

1. BODY SWAP 4 HIRE. From the story - The Donor.

Q1. How much would you pay to pocess a rock/Hip hop stars body for a weekend. He is famous, He's rich and he has a hot glamour model partner?

2. KNIGHTMARE PREVENTION - From the story Spoilers.

This tech is designed to monitor brainwaves, It recognises the signs of an impending nightmare then it redirects the unsubconcious mind away from nightmare destinations.

3. PLANTERIAN/ TERROFORMING. From the sci fi story - Exodus.

This story focused on political motivation. A new Earth has been found. Will wealthy people one day want to leave Earth in the hope of prospering beyond middle and lower classes?

4. THE SHOCKWAVE CONSOLE. From the scifi story - Shockwave.

No more random violent digital killings? Instead gamers will kill diseases which will be dressed up as characters in a computer games.

5. THE LOADSTONE DEVICE. From the sci fi story - The Wire.

The concept of recognising the missing link as a independent organism. The next aim is to controll the evolutionary process within all animals and plants. Eventually mankind will try to turn daffodils into roses at the push of a button.

6. Taking Pets.

7. (E)foods. - From the story - Not of this Earth. N.O.T.E.

The concept of making Human food from direct atoms. However it turns Humans into zombies.

8. AFTERBIRTH ABORTITIONS. From the sci fi story - Abort.

In the future children will be aborted, Even after birth, Especially if they're orphans.

9. ANTI MATTER TECH - From the sci fi story N.O.T.E. Not of this earth.

This tech is used on roads. It alters hard substances until any object of mass can pass straight through it. This tech eliminates traffic jams and accidents.

10. TELEPORTATION.

11. ARTIFICAL WOMB FARMING/ THE CHARKRAS TENT. From the sci fi story Access point one.

It simply Magatises organic material including skin. Curing Hemophiacs diseases. Unfortunately it then indivertibly allows evil dead humans to raise and regain a physical form.

First he waters his plant then he gets dressed.

Decklan is class president. He in all of most subjects. It's a normal day apart from the obvious. Amy hasn't told anyone about his increase intelligence. The form teacher Mr Hudson. He tells them about the up coming fancy dress party.

Restaurant.

Dwayne orders a glass of Cola. Amy orders a glass of Cola too. Everything is normal apart from the fact they're being served by a Robot. There are 3 Robots in the Restaurant. They all look identical to glamour model Kim East. These Robots refuse to serve costumers who place an order in English. The A.I Robot was invented by an Englishman. Non English speaking Nations stole his A.I idea.

If your a victim of a crime, You call the Police. However the Police refuse to investigate crimes to English speaking people.

Amy and Dwayne go for a walk in the park. They start kissing. A Policeman interupts them. He says "Comment tappelles-tu?" Dwayne says profitaient du temps. The Policeman asks Amy "quel âge as-tu?" She doesn't know how to speak in French. The Policeman laughs, He asks again. Dwayne answers the Policeman. "elle a 18 ans." The Policeman leaves them to it.

Amy asks Dwayne "How have you suddenly learnt how to speak in French?" She asks "Why do I think your holding out on me? If you hold out on me i'll hold out with you." He tells her he's got superpowers due to the recent Shockwave. "Lets not talk here." He takes her to his room. All the rooms are 5 star. All as tidy as a showroom.

Dwayne shows Amy Jones his other inventions. He's built a machine that can reduce the size or increase the size of any object. He extends his bottle of Beer, Several times.

Once home he shows her his Teleporter. They Teleport all over the World. Hong Kong, China, Sydney Australia, New York U.S.A. It's Friday night so she wants to party. She tells Dwayne to put on her favorite playlist. Dwayne has internet access. It isn't long before she wants to go to New York Cities night hotspots. She's only 18 but that's old enough for a girl who's high of life. She parties all night.

3:00 am.

Amy still sleeps with her talking doll, May. The next Morning Dwayne tell's her he can turn toy's into A.I dolls who have independent thoughts. He asks if she wants him to do it with May. Amy says yes.

Earth Parallel - 2 - Blip.

He copies as much tech as he can. Which includes the Hollotrails app. Once installed the Idealman.com app immediatly points out every girl who fancies him. Decklan receives an Advert.

The Mircule Pill.

When your will is over the hill
All you need is the Mircule pill.

Earth Parallel - 2 -

A Female Computer Voice. Mircule Pill.

The Miracle pill is designed to take the guess work out of achieving an Organism. The pill ensures that you and your partner will achieve a climax at an exact moment.

The Miracle pill directs the chemicals that create the orgasmic sensation. It also has a built in anabolic steroid that grants the Male user instant recovery from ejaculation, Ensuring that he will instantly be able to restart sexural intercourse again immediately after achieving an orgasm.

The Miracle pill will ensure you can automatically achieve an orgasm depending on which pill he has taken. Dosages arrive in a 10 minute. 30 minute and 1 hour pill.

The Burst Miracle Pill.

This unisex pill allows both parties to climax from a single penetrative stroke.

ALWAY ALWAYS READ THE LABEL.

Monday - University.

Dwayne Finds a stray Puppy. Fortunately he has his mobile DIY kit. It consists of spear parts. eg.

1. A MOBILE PHONE -
2. ARTIFICAL WOMB FARMING/ THE CHARKRAS TENT -
3. AFTERBIRTH ABORTITIONS -

It takes 10 minutes to make a device that is able to make the Puppy talk......in English. That's thanks to his special collar. Dwayne carries it home even though student's aren't allowed pets. He can always make it invisible. He names his Dog, Willy. Dwayne tells Willy "Never talk in front of strangers."

7:00 pm.

Dwayne has turned his Cactus into a Marijuwana plant. He looks at himself in a mirror. He says "I can't loose. Amy coughs, Dwayne thinks Amy is telling him off for being too arrogant. However he soon realises Amy is ill.

Diseases That Are Hard To Diagnose.

1. Irritable Bowel Syndrome.
2. Celiac Disease.

3. Appendicitis.
4. Hyperthyroidism.
5. Beta - anemia.

Beta - anemia.

She's had it for all her life. It's an Hereditary disease. He thinks It's not serious. He uses his Chemistry set to cure her. There's a knock on the door.

It's Mr Decklan the Teacher, The Italian Teacher. He talks about the English Language. Mr Decklan says "Imagine being immortal" He speaks in the English Language " Dwayne says "posso aiutarla?" Which means How can I help you? Mr Decklans says it becomes a curse. Did you know immortals can't sleep....never....ever. That's why we are the way we are. I'm 56 years old. Dwayne was about to make certain animals and his Marijuwana Plants Immortal. He says "Your only able to speak in the English language. You lost your culture. Slavery is to blame. In comparison Indian and a Pakistan are multi lingual."

10:00 Earth's Parallel. The Aura Trail.

First of all Dwanye creates the Aura Trail. It is a sutle trace of energy which we all leave behind. It's simular to a slugs trail of mucus. A teleportation device called the Aura Trail is used as a form of transport. Each Trail is different so the Police will use it to solve crimes. Dwanye Summons Kim East. He only talks to her for a minute. He can't believe it worked.

Earth Parallel - The Devils Alter.

Dwayne copies the Loadstone Project. It means he can change the DNA of any animal or plant. He can change a cat into a dog and turn a Human into a Tree. He also copies the Devils Alter. This means he can controll the weather.

An English Wedding.

Dwayne proposes to Amy. Amy she accepts his hand in marriage. She wants to tell everyone but Dwanye says "Lets keep it as a secret. Only invite the people we trust." English Weddings are illegal. They will be killed if the Police catches them. They have to organise a safe place. We need a Priest.

Father Luke Ham.

He openly talks in English. However he talks the word of the Bible. Dwayne asks Father Ham to marry him and Amy. Father Ham says "Non English speaking people are powerful...... Beyond Words. They have Time Machines, Teleportation Devices etc. Their invisible, So they could be listening/Watching us right now. It's not an invasion. They're not on their way here, There already here." Dwayne beggs and beggs and beggs. Eventually Father Ham accepts the job.

There's Something In The Air.

Mr Decklan is a Spy. He has been pretending to be sympathetic to the English speaking Language. Mark Flowers spoke in English when talking to Mr Decklan aka the new Teacher. Dwayne and Amy decide to change the date of the Wedding to 17th of July.

Raid.

Dwayne's room is raided and trashed. The Teachers are there because Dwayne's grades at School has risen 70% in a Month. The French Teacher, Hank Wells asks "How have you become so good in such a short space of time? "Dwayne says Je prétendais." I was pretending. "je parle couramment français."

Amy préfère les hommes intelligent

Amy prefers Men who are intelligent.

The Teachers take away Dwayne's DIY kit. But that night Dwayne dismantles his TV and he dismantles his stereo. He builds a device to see if his room is bugged. He gets the all clear. He turns himself invisible. He walks straight through the locked door. He takes his dismantled gadgets back and changes them with rubbish. He reduces his DIY kit to the size of a one pound coin.

Sunday.

Amy is super intelligent. She isn't at Dwayne level. Mainly because it wasn't tech that made Dwayne super intelligent, It was the Shockwave.

Monday - A Boring Day.

Amy is visiting her Parents - Northing on TV and that includes the Internet.

Tuesday -

It's raining.

Wednesday -

No football on TV.

News.

It's The Wedding Day.

Dwayne builds a Weather Machine. The Weather Machine works. This means his Wedding Day will be Hot. Amy has come back from her Parents. Everything and Everyone is ready. The only issue is they have to pay a toll once they enter Birmingham.

Convergence.

The Wedding is held in a Synagogue. It only last 30 minutes. As far as anyone else is concerned, They won't have an Honeymoon. However Amy and Dwayne know they will be going to Spain for a Week. It took 1.30 hours. Before it took 20 hours a 46 minutes. They land to a news Flash story. Spain Invade - Portugal.

Dwayne's Toy House.

Dwayne's bedroom is bigger.......much bigger on the inside than it is on the outside. Censor cheque switch on soon as the door is touch. So he won't be caught. Being invisible won't help either.

The Million Man March - The Freedom Community.

This won't be anything like the American Million Man March in 1995. It's for all races. Plus it's in March. March has a good ring to it The English Language protesters start to loot. They throw petrol Bombs throw shop windows. The Police try not to get involved until the Robot Police make a move. Most the Robot Police look Identical to Martin Luther king or Gandhi. Others look like Malcolm X, George Washington and Nelson Mandela.

No Mercy.

The protesters start to turn their aggression on the Robots. The law says Robots can defend themselves from attack. They can even use lethal force. There's an all out war between protesters and Robot Cops. Robots shoot without thought. Dwayne opens his DIY kit. He tries to build a over ride machine. He switches it on. The Robots switch off and they drop their guns to the ground. He gives his over ride Gadget to a little Girl. The Robot was going to kill her. Because she was openly talking in English.

The News.

Late reports inform viewers that the Robots killed over 500 people. No Police where seriously hurt.

Amy Jones vs The Miracle pill.

First, Dwayne checks to see if the Worlds most expensive Hotel is available. It's fully booked but it will be available in a year's time. Dwayne books it. He rebuilds a Teleporter and his Time Machine. He and Amy arrive in Italy. 9:00 am, one year in the future.

Advertisement Channel. The Miracle Pill.

ALWAYS ALWAYS READ THE LABEL.

Dwayne pours two glasses of Champagne and climbs into the four poster bed. He materialises the pill into Amy's hand. She doesn't hesitate for a second. She swallows it. She punches him on the arm. Amy says "No one can be this sexy. They kiss for a while and then they start to make love.

The End.

CHAPTER SIX

UNLEASHED

Notoriously high maintance actress, Kerry Stunns except the role in the Movie "unlimited" Their are rumours that she will demand a new extension to her 12 bedroom Mansion. The 23 year old has been offered 15 million pounds for the lead role as character kelly Hannon.

Wetting The Bed.

8 year old Roy Sydney has wet the bed many times. His Mum, Brenda tells her Husband, Glenn to take the mattress to the landfill site. Their going to buy a new mattress. This time they will keep the plastic cover on it. Brenda is a Graphic Designer. She lives in a Flat in Altrincham. Brenda sees Roy's new mattress. It gives her an idea for a cartoon character. Snip the annoying bedbug.

Tabitha Racley.

Her boob size has returned to normal. Most of the time she was glad with it but every so often she misses them. Captain Johnny is Car jacked. He beggs the thief's not to steel his Comic and they don't but that's only because one of them is a comic book fan.

Johnny take Tabitha camping. Meanwhile the Terrorist group Fetch strikes again. They destroy the underground goverment base. Only one Police officer survives. His name is Porter.

Johnny is reading Hannah his new comic. Suddenly they hear someone outside.

Shockwave.

There's a Laboratory in a Goverment Base it's known as the epi Center. Johnny worked there.

The Shockwave crisis has been cured for some time. No one has powers anymore. Carol Nash says "People needs science fiction." There's a new Cosmic fiction book out. Written by Captain Johnny himself. He's created a new villian for his latest edition of his Comic. It's a female character called the Mirror Maiden. She can steel powers from super hero's.

Captain Johnny Zero and Tabitha Zero are on a camping trip. There are several other campers on the site. They hear and feel an Earthquake. They're curious so they both leave the tent. But they see northing strange.

The Preventors.

Captain Johnny Zero and Tabitha Zero are on a camping trip. There are several other campers on the site. They hear and feel an Earthquake. They're curious so they both leave the tent. But they see northing strange.

The Preventors - Meanwhile.

It's them who have been blocking the Shockwave signal. The Policeman called Porter recognises Johnny Zero. He's the only survivor from a Earthquake which in fact was a Terrorist attack. He asks Johnny and Hannah to help him search the area for people who have been affected by the Shockwave.

Tabitha asks "So everyone who had powers before will regain them. And new people will gain new powers?" "Yes" says Porter. Back ups on it's way. However other Police Officers will be dealing with their own problems. They go to Kitten Street. Tabitha Zero starts to grow again. Porter shoots her with his Normalised.

Lance Ryder.

They drive around the City until they see a line of Women out side a House. They've all come to tell a 16 year boy their desperately in love with him. Lance Ryder's Mother is trying to turn the rampant Women away from her home. Porter interviews her Son for a short while. Lance beggs Porter not to take his Powers away. Porter apologise and then he shoots Lance with his Normaliser. It's clearly a Shockwave incident.

Meanwhile.

It's them who have been blocking the Shockwave signal. The Policeman called Porter recognises Johnny Zero. He's the only survivor from a Earthquake which in fact was a Terrorist attack. He asks Johnny and Hannah to help him search the area for people who have been affected by the Shockwave.

Tabitha asks "So everyone who had powers before will regain them. And new people will gain new powers?" "Yes" say's Porter. Back ups on it's way. However other Police Officers will be dealing with their own problems. They go to Kitten Street. Tabitha Zero starts to grow again. Porter shoots her with his Normalised.

Lance Ryder.

They drive around the City until they see a line of Women out side a House. They've all come to tell a 16 year boy their desperately in love with him. Lance Ryder's Mother is trying to turn the rampant Women away from her home. Porter interviews her Son for a short while. Lance beggs Porter not to take his Powers away. Porter apologiser's and then he shoots Lance with his Normaliser. It's clearly a Shockwave incident.

Porter received a text. He tells Johnny and Tabitha they have 7 hours to get as many people as they can. He won't be able to turn them normal again after the watershed. They head for Spark Road.

The Next Morning.

Snip the bedbug is alive. Brenda instantly knows it's the Shockwave. She'll have to tell people he is a screensaver

Shockwave.

Brenda was in bed, Working on her new cartoon characters, The bedbugs. Before bed she tells Snip not to talk to anyone else but her. Snip says "OK." He says "To a real bedbug a mattress is a country." Brenda threw away her Son's old mattress. She closes Snip's folder and opens Tie, The bedbug eater folder. He says I don't mean to be spoilt but do you realise i've been naked all this time don't you?

Meanwhile.

Porter suggests they separate. He gives Johnny a Normaliser Gun. He says "It steals and gives powers. Don't ever give anyone powers. Not even yourself. Under no circumstances. Is that clear?" Johnny nods.

Another Shockwave - The Invisible Man.

Johnny and Tabitha are taking on an Invisible Man. Johnny shoots at the invisible Man but he misses. The invisible Man punches and kick Johnny. Pokes and prods Tabitha. Suddenly their helped by a super flying Police Dog. Johnny shoots the invisible bank robber with his Normaliser. The dog catches her.

The bank robber is a Woman. Johnny lets the Superdog fly her to the nearest Police Station. Meanwhile a giant animal is reeking havoc in Sale.

The Jeweller.

He touches a stone and it turns into a diamond. The Jeweller touches another stone, It turns into Ruby. Porter has the app that finds abnormal readings. Porter walks into his shop. The Jeweller says "look at what I can do." Porter says "Sorry ole chap." He shoots him with the Normaliser.

The Sketch Artist.

Ian tells his best friend, Paul he feels different. "The way I use to feel." He phones his Boss and tells him he's ready to come back into work. A Woman has been kidnapped. Ian's eyes go black. He draws as if he's being controlled. He draws several landscapes. He draws the kidnappers faces. He even draws the Living room. Porter walks into interview room 4. He asks Ian "Do you have powers?" Ian says "Yes but i'm no villain." Porter shoots Ian with his Normaliser

Prestwich.

Tabitha and Johnny prepare to kill the giant Monster. But other Agents delt with the situation before they got there. Tabitha and Johnny start to hunt others who are attacking the City.

A blind Man can cure baldness. Johnny shoots him with his Normaliser.

This 35 year old Man has been given best voice in the World. He sings several songs. Porter shoots him with his Normaliser. Neither Porter or Johnny apprehended the Shockwave victims

Brenda's Shopping.

Tie has started to gain controll of Brenda's Laptop. He travels from the Laptop to an electric billboard. His size grows exponentially. Once there, He attacks the Houses large or small. The People who make waste.

Brenda has an Idea. She opens Snips folder. She goes on and on about Tie and it's all her fault. Snip shouts "Shut up." He believes she can draw him any weapon. Brenda draws a raygun and a Shield. Brenda tries using a rubber. Tie says that'll be like using a rubber on a photograph

Tabitha - Mirror Maiden.

Johnny finished, Copied and saved his Comic that night after the Car Jacking incident. The Mirror Maiden is copied from Tabitha. It's Jhonny's turn to use the Normaliser. There's a Man who can grow infinitely. Amazingly Tabitha steals his Powers without the Normaliser. She doesn't know what to do. She hunts for any one who has been affected by the Shockwave.

Brenda sends Snip into the billboard. He disposes of Tie within a Minute. All he needed was his raygun. Brenda apologizes. Snip says "For what?" Brenda says your naked. Snip says "i'm a bedbug......i'm supposed to be naked."

Johnny has an idea. He will rewrite the Comic inorder to stop Tabitha from copying powers. It works. Porter and Johnny catch up with Tabitha. She has stolen the powers from a Man who could fly. Porter shoots his normaliser. However Tabitha has created a Normaliser reflector. Porter says "There's only one other option. She gets her powers from you." He shoots Captain Johnny zero in the head. Tabitha falls from the sky. She's lost all her powers.

10 Minutes Before The Shockwave/Aftershock

Is Irreversible.

Porter heads back to the epi centre. He confronts the Boss, Carol Nash. She confesses her support for the Shockwave. "This was the only way to generate the energy that we needed to make certain projects start. Carol is using the Normaliser. She uses it once every minute. 60 seconds.

The New Life Project.

"C.G.I. Graphic designers will one day be like Gods. Snip, Tie and Tabitha are results of this project." She shoots herself with the Normaliser.

Preventing Evolution.

She shoots herself with the Normaliser again. "She says "Being Human is out of date. The aim is to prevent Humans from evolving into something that isn't humane." Porter has no need to challenge Carol. He simply shoots her with the Normaliser.

Hospital.

Tabitha wakes, She has a broken arm and a broken leg. Porter stole the powers of an immortal Man. He used it to bring him back alive.

A Month Later.

Kerry Stunns is in the Movie called "Perish" She's the star and she still gets paid even though she plays no part on the Movie. She only appears via C.G.I. Hugh Smith explains this is the future of Hollywood. We have always had characters that weren't real. Cartoons. Today we all could be fans of Famous people who are long dead or never ever really existed at all.

Snip is the same size as all bedbugs. He has been allowed to live. He's found a new home. He's Friends and Family are now living in Buckingham Palace. They throw a moving in Party. Blue Blood Buffet...all you can eat.

The End.

Shockwave – The English Language.

INTRODUCTION

C.*

If u ws in the big brother house.
I wud'nt vote u out.
I'm turnin ova.
If ur goin – I'm goin 2.

V1.

The radio's on.

It's time 4 me blow up again – I'm worse than an air balloons.
I care about Lyrics more than chefs care about food.

N i still dnt give fork - A Knife or a Spoon.
N ive been kickin it this way since i ws in the womb.

All u gotta do is absorb it.
Im runnin the run nt jus walkin n talkin.

Turn the base up until the clubs dance floor ---(boun - cies).
N u start 2 feel all ---- at sea.

Im nt talkin 2 the nt on the 1st nite u.
Im talkin 2 the YOU who will make man wait a whole month or 2.

Im talkin 2 that party animal - U hide away.

Who sings n dances 2 weekend songs on a weekday.

C.*

If u ws in the big brother house.
I wud'nt vote u out.
Im turnin ova.
If ur goin - Im goin 2.

V2.*

You remind me of ripe fruit.
Ur so sexy u left my lips loose.

It's all about u - Period.
N im the no.1 seed at this but i weren't grown in dirt

Theres no U TURNS once u fall in love.
N ur so hot Antiperparant ante enuff

Weve had more than 1 awkward --- Situation.
N a 101 of sexy --- conversations

N i got more songs than Dalmatians.
So u cnt dance in front of me without me tryin it on.

I dnt pay any attention 2 half of the things i say.
Bt i thank god that ur dad were'nt gay.

Vb.*

Your lites camera action smile - Is a kin 2 a master piece.
That's frm my eyes n my hearts p.o.v.

The whole world frames u.
U got taste 2 - N i want more of ur kisses - If there still on the menu.

C.

If u ws in the big brother house.
I wud'nt vote u out.
Im turnin ova.
If ur goin - Im goin 2.

V3.

U stand on a dance floor with 1 foot on its chest.
With more eyes on u than - the internet.

Bt im feastin my eyes on u - n im nt goin ona diet.
Still u - Even if a gun ws fired.

1 flash frm u will start a Mexican wave.
Bt pullin u is harder than brakin in2 safes.

If u won't - LET ME - dance with both hands around ur waste.
I'll cry so many tears - you wondered if she ws - made 4 Mermaids.

Grab ur coat you've pulled - ill get my str8 jacket.
I cn pt my hands in BT UR gonna ave 2 tie it frm the bk end.

If ur mine all mine ill buy u a new coat 4 ur birthday.
Real fur if it lands on a Thursday.

V.b.

All i cn give u is - love n romance. even appollogised if i eva make you
cry - In advance.

Ur an artists dream.
Ur smilin eye' - Is the sweetest thing ive eva seen.

C.*

If u ws in the big brother house.
I wud'nt vote u out.
Im turnin ova.
If ur goin - Im goin 2.

THE END.

Printed in the United States
by Baker & Taylor Publisher Services